WHAT DO I SAY ABOUT THAT?

...COPING WITH AN INCARCERATED PARENT

published by

National Center for Youth Issues
Practical Guidance Resources
Educators Can Trust
ncyi.org
www.ncyi.org

This book is dedicated in loving memory of Mrs. Clara Ward.

Her deep love and concern for children of incarcerated parents was evident to all who knew her.

Duplication and Copyright

No part of this publication may be reproduced, stored in a retrieval system or transmitted in any form by any means, electronic, mechanical, photocopy, recording or otherwise without prior written permission from the publisher except for all worksheets and activities which may be reproduced for a specific group or class. Reproduction for an entire school or school district is prohibited.

National Center for Youth Issues

Practical Guidance Resources
Educators Can Trust

ncyi.org

P.O. Box 22185
Chattanooga, TN 37422-2185
423.899.5714 • 866.318.6294
fax: 423.899.4547 • www.ncyi.org

ISBN: 978-1-937870-37-9
© 2015 National Center for Youth Issues, Chattanooga, TN
All rights reserved.
Written by: Julia Cook
Illustrations by: Anita DuFalla
Design by: Phillip W. Rodgers
Contributing Editor: Beth Spencer Rabon
Published by National Center for Youth Issues • Softcover
Printed at Starkey Printing, Chattanooga, Tennessee, U.S.A., June 2016

My dad's in the slammer. At least that's what people say.

What they really mean is,
he's in jail because
he lost his way.

He made a bad decision.
Actually more like three or four.
And now he's serving five to ten,
and it might be even more.

It stinks not to have my dad around, and it makes me **really mad**.

Sometimes I start to miss him a lot, and then I feel **really bad**.

I have no idea **what to say** about that.

5

My dad says that drugs and alcohol made him choose to do the wrong things.

But he could have said **NO** to the drugs and the booze, then my life wouldn't be what it seems.

Why didn't he love us enough to say **NO**?

Aren't we worth it to him?

He had a choice...

us or drugs.

HE CHOSE

to let the drugs win.

Last week my mom said, "We have to move because I just can't pay the bills."

Now I'm starting my sixth school in just three years.
Does she have any idea how that feels?

When other kids ask me about my dad,
I say he lives out of town.

If they knew about the slammer,
they might start putting me down.

JOE'S HARDWARE

How do I tell them my dad's in jail,
or what caused his arrest?

When I see other kids with their dads,
I start to get depressed.

"WHY ME?"

I ask.

It's just **NOT FAIR**.

Now I'm
without
my dad!

Sometimes I feel
like I'm all alone,
and it makes me
really sad.

I have no idea
what to say
about that.

My mom is doing the best she can to take care of my brother and me.

She says, "I just can't wait for the day when your daddy gets set free."

Sometimes her face is full of fear but she always says, "I'm just fine."

Her eyes are so red because she cries a lot, and she's tired all the time.

13

"Aren't you angry at Dad?" I ask.
"He did bad things and chose to do drugs!"

"And now he's trying hard to do better.
Come here and I'll give you a hug."

I have no idea **what to say** about that.

Sometimes we go
to visit my dad,
and I see myself
in his eyes.

Then my anger
builds up inside me,
and I almost
start to cry.

Then I start to
feel scared inside
because I know
that I'm half him.

What if I do
the things he has done
and end up
where he has been?

I look around and see other kids who are visiting their dads.
I wonder if they feel like I do…and then I start to get mad!

"IT'S NOT FAIR,

I scream,

that you're in here and I don't have a dad!"

I HATE to come to the slammer!

It makes me feel so sad!

My dad has no idea **what to say** about that.

Today I found a note in my pocket.
It was from my dad.

Dear Sun,

I made won bad chois ~~wh~~
witch made me make a lot
more of them. You ar strong.
You r good on the inside. I can
see that in your eyes. Don't get
eatun by drugs and booz. Listn
to me. Be better than me. Work hard
in school. Don't just do eezy.

I love you son.
Just becuz I let you
doun duzn't give you
permission to hurt yourself.
Win at you're life. Every
thing you do counts. —Dad

SOLVE: $4-(-5+8)$

$(-5+8)=3$

$4-3=1$

$8x+19x-6y-(-y)$

$8x+19x-$

$27x-$

My mom says the slammer
is helping my dad.

He's starting to see why his
choices were bad.

It's teaching him how
to play by the rules.

They're even letting him
go back to school.

I hope he can turn
his life around.

And get out of the slammer
and stand on free ground.

I read my letter almost every day.

I'm hoping his words will show me the way.

Today when I saw him he looked into my eyes.

I could see right away they were filled up with **TRY**.

And then he started
to talk to me.
He said,

"Son I have
shown you who
NOT to be."

I had no idea
what to say
about that.

My dad has his battles, and I have mine.

And I know that to win them, it's gonna take time.

It is what it is, and if I make a mistake,

I will pay the price for the choices I make.

WRONG WAY

RIGHT WAY

I know I can't change the way things are now,
but I know my dad loves me, and he's showing me how …

To make better choices in all that I do.
He's doing his best, and I'll do that too.

And that's all I can say...

TIPS FOR HELPING A CHILD WITH AN INCARCERATED PARENT

When a loved one is sentenced to prison, the emotional turmoil is difficult for everyone to handle. Children of incarcerated parents often suffer the heaviest burden of all. These kids pay the price of hardship, and as a result often develop mental health issues such as depression, anxiety, post-traumatic stress disorder, and feelings of abandonment and grief. Here are a few tips that might help to improve this difficult situation:

- Be honest when explaining the situation. Honesty builds trust, which is crucial to every human relationship – "Daddy has moved to a place called "prison" or "jail." He is going to live there for a while. Sometimes when grown-ups make bad choices and break laws, they have to move to prison. Prison will help daddy learn how to make better choices."

- Help your child feel more secure by surrounding him with people and places with which he is familiar. If possible, try not overwhelm your child with new places and unfamiliar people right away.

- Create a predictable schedule for your child each day and stick closely to it. Being able to predict and plan events that will occur throughout the day will help ease the anxious feelings of being out of control of the current situation. Children perform best when they know what to expect. Routine is priceless!

- Take time each day to ask your child how they are feeling and validate those feelings -"I can only imagine what you might be going through. I feel that way too sometimes, " etc. Reassure your children that it's ok to talk about and express their feelings, regardless of what or how big they are.

- Let your child know that the incarceration is NOT his/her fault. Some children will inadvertently blame themselves for their parent's incarceration which leads to severe feelings of anxiety and guilt.

- If possible, maintain consistent contact with the incarcerated parent through phone calls and visits etc. In advance, explain to the child what the visit might look like: "We can't sit next to mommy, but we can see her through the glass and talk to her over the phone," etc. When calling an incarcerated parent, it may be helpful to have the child write down a list of things to talk about prior to making the call.

- Take care of yourself! It is very difficult to care for others, especially children if you "let yourself go." Take time out at least once a day to relax or do something that **YOU** enjoy.

Meet Julia!!

NATIONAL LEVEL SPEAKER,
AWARD-WINNING AUTHOR,
EDUCATOR, AND FORMER
SCHOOL COUNSELOR

Julia Cook, MS has authored over seventy children's books that address issues such as social/life-skills, self-care, electronic device etiquette/safety, and more!

Visit **ncyi.org/juliacook** for more details!

National Center for Youth Issues
ncyi.org
Practical Guidance Resources
Educators Can Trust

HOME OF

Storybook Central